When Winter Comes

by Russell Freedman

pictures by Pamela Johnson

A Smart Cat Book

E. P. Dutton   New York

Text copyright © 1981 by Russell Freedman
Illustrations copyright © 1981 by Pamela Johnson

Library of Congress Cataloging in Publication Data

Freedman, Russell.   When winter comes.
(A Smart cat book)
Summary: Describes how various animals prepare for
and survive the winter season.
1. Winter—Juvenile literature.
2. Animals, Habits and behavior of—Juvenile literature.
[1. Winter.   2. Animals—Habits and behavior]
I. Johnson, Pamela.   II. Title.   III.Series.
QH81.F825   1981   591.54'3   80-22831   ISBN 0-525-42583-7

Published in the United States by Elsevier-Dutton
Publishing Co., Inc., 2 Park Avenue, New York, N.Y. 10016

Published simultaneously in Canada by Clarke,
Irwin & Company Limited, Toronto and Vancouver

Editor: Ann Troy   Designer: Claire Counihan

Printed in the U.S.A.   First Edition
10   9   8   7   6   5   4   3   2   1

Contents

Where Are the Animals?   5

Saving Food for Winter   8

Sleeping Through Winter   18

Busy All Winter   27

Leaving Winter Behind   36

Where Are the Animals?

The woods seem quiet on a winter day. When you walk, you can hear the crunch, crunch, crunch of your feet in the snow.

Are any animals in the woods? You may not see them, but animals are all around.

Up in a tree, a squirrel peeks from a hole. Under the ground, a woodchuck sleeps. Behind a tree, a white rabbit hides in the snow.

For animals, winter can be hard. How do they find food? How do they keep warm? How do they stay alive when winter comes?

Saving Food for Winter

In summer, squirrels can find lots of food. They eat fruits, green plants and small insects. Sometimes they take peas or beans from a farmer's field.

Summer is easy, a time to grow fat. In winter, food will be hard to find. Squirrels get ready for winter by saving nuts.

When nuts grow ripe, the squirrels get busy. They look for all kinds of nuts. With their teeth, they cut nuts from trees and let them drop to the ground.

They eat a few nuts right away. But they save most of their nuts for the cold days ahead.

Gray squirrels bury their nuts. A squirrel digs a hole with its paws. It picks up a nut with its teeth and drops it in the hole. Then it covers the nut with earth.

Each nut has its own hole. Soon the squirrel has buried hundreds of nuts in the ground.

When winter comes, the squirrel lives
in a hole high up in a tree. It sleeps
in the hole at night, away from the wind
and snow. When it wants to eat, it runs
down to the ground. It pushes away the
snow and digs up a nut. It has saved
enough nuts to last until spring.

Beavers also save food for winter. They save tree branches.

A family of beavers works together. They cut down trees with their orange teeth. They bite off the branches. Then they carry the branches to their house in the middle of a pond.

The beavers keep the branches in a pile next to their house. Soon the pile of wood reaches above the water.

In winter, ice covers the beavers' pond. Snow covers their house.

When a beaver is hungry, it slips out of the house and swims under the ice. It grabs a branch from the food pile and carries it home. Then it nibbles at the bark, as though it were eating corn on the cob. That's all it eats while winter lasts.

Sleeping Through Winter

A woodchuck doesn't save food. It stops eating when winter comes. It sleeps all winter long.

Before winter, the woodchuck eats a lot. It stuffs itself with grass. The more it eats, the fatter it gets.

On the first cold day, the woodchuck
squeezes through a tunnel. The tunnel
leads to an underground den with four
or five rooms.

The woodchuck goes to its bedroom.
It closes the door with dirt. It wraps its
tail around its head and falls asleep on
a bed of grass.

It sleeps so deeply, it almost seems
dead. Its breathing slows down. Its body
becomes cold and stiff. If you touched
the woodchuck, it wouldn't wake up. It
might seem dead, but it's not. Its extra
fat keeps it alive. Its body uses the fat
for food.

The woodchuck sleeps all winter long. It may sleep six months without eating. When it wakes in the spring and leaves its den, it is a very skinny woodchuck.

Sleeping through winter is called hibernation (hy-ber-NAY-shun). Ground squirrels and chipmunks also hibernate (HY-ber-nate), just like woodchucks.

Bears also sleep in the winter, but
not as deeply. They often sleep in caves.
On warm days, they wake up. They go
outside and look for something to eat.
When it gets cold again, they go back to
their caves and sleep some more.

In the north, animals like frogs, turtles and snakes hibernate. Frogs dig into the mud at the bottom of ponds, where they sleep the winter away. Turtles dig holes in the ground. Snakes crawl into deep, dark caves.

Sometimes hundreds of snakes sleep through winter together, rolled up in a big ball.

Some insects hibernate too. When it gets cold, they look for places to hide. They crawl under stones and logs. They creep into holes. They dig under the bark of trees. Then they stop moving until winter is gone.

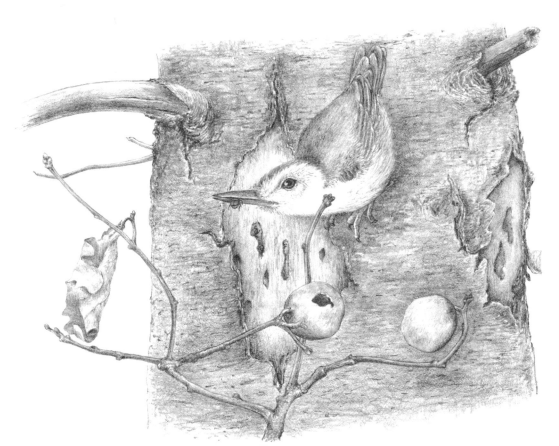

Busy All Winter

Some animals sleep through winter and never go out in the cold. Others stay busy. They know where to look for food when snow covers the ground.

A red fox hunts for its food. It hunts through fields and woods for rabbits and mice. The fox sleeps in the snow with its nose under its tail. Its fur coat keeps it warm.

A meadow mouse hides from the fox. It builds a winter nest of dry grass. Snow falls and covers the nest. To find food, the mouse digs tunnels through the snow. It runs through the tunnels and looks for seeds and roots to eat.

Rabbits eat bark and twigs in winter.
They sleep under bushes or in rocky dens
where they can't be seen.

30

The snowshoe rabbit changes color every year. Its summer coat is brown. Its winter coat is snow white, so it can hide from enemies.

Its name comes from the long hairs on its back feet. In winter, these hairs act as snowshoes. They keep the rabbit from sinking into soft snow.

Deer change color too. Their summer
coats are brown. Their thick winter coats
are grayish brown, like the winter woods.
They spend the winter together in herds,
looking for food in the woods.

Deer eat the bark and twigs of trees as far up as they can reach. They paw at the snow to find nuts and weeds. At night, they tramp down the snow to make their beds.

Birds in the north must search hard
for food. They grow extra feathers for
winter. On cold days, they fluff out
their feathers and pull in their necks.

Leaving Winter Behind

Winter is a hard time for birds. They don't mind the cold weather, because their feathers keep them warm. But they have a hard time getting enough to eat.

Some birds stay in the north all winter.
Blue jays hunt for nuts in the snow.
Woodpeckers cut into trees with their
strong beaks. They dig under the bark
and eat hibernating insects.

Other birds can't find enough food in winter. When the days grow shorter, they fly south. In the south, food is easy to find.

Robins fly south to warm places like Florida. Ducks may spend the winter in Mexico. Barn swallows fly all the way from Canada to South America.

How do these birds find their way?
They watch the sun and the stars move
across the sky. The sun and the stars
tell them which way to go.

Many kinds of birds fly south each fall. In spring, they fly north again. This is called migration (my-GRAY-shun). It means to move from one place to another at a certain time of year.

Some insects migrate, just like birds. They join in large groups and fly south. You may have seen black-and-orange monarch butterflies going south in the fall. Thousands of monarchs may fly south together.

As winter ends in the north, the days grow longer. The sun gets stronger. Woodchucks and ground squirrels wake up. Insects crawl out of their hiding places. Snow melts, and plants grow everywhere. The woods in the spring are green and alive.

Soon the first birds return. They come
flying in over the treetops. Now they can
find plenty of food in the north.

If you watch the sky on a spring day, you may see birds flying north. Many people watch for them. When the birds come back, we know that winter is really over.

INDEX

barn swallows, 38
bears, 22
beavers, 14–16
birds, 35
    migration of, 36–42,
        46–47
blue jays, 37
butterflies, 42

chipmunks, 21
colors of animals,
        changes in, 31, 32

deer, 32–33
ducks, 38

enemies, hiding from,
        28–31

food:
    hibernation and,
        18–20
    looking for, 11, 22,
        27–28, 32–35,
        37–38
    saving of, 8–16
foxes, 27–28

frogs, 24

gray squirrels, 12–13
ground squirrels, 21, 44

hibernation, 18–25

insects, 8, 25, 37, 42,
        44

meadow mouse, 28
mice, 27, 28
migration, 38–47

rabbits, 6, 27, 30, 31
red fox, 27–28
robins, 38

snakes, 24–25
snowshoe rabbits, 31
squirrels, 6–13, 21, 44
swallows, 38

turtles, 24

white rabbit, 6
woodchucks, 6, 18–21,
        44
woodpeckers, 37